Wish

Quarto is the authority on a wide range of topics.
Quarto educates, entertains and enriches the lives of
our readers—enthusiasts and lovers of hands-on living.
www.quartoknows.com

First Published in 2019 by words & pictures,
an imprint of The Quarto Group.
The Old Brewery, 6 Blundell Street,
London N7 9BH, United Kingdom.
T (0)20 7700 6700 F (0)20 7700 8066
www.quartoknows.com

A catalogue record for this book is available from the British Library.

ISBN: 978-1-78603-345-1

9 8 7 6 5 4 3 2 1

Manufactured in Shenzhen, China HH102018

Wish

Chris Saunders

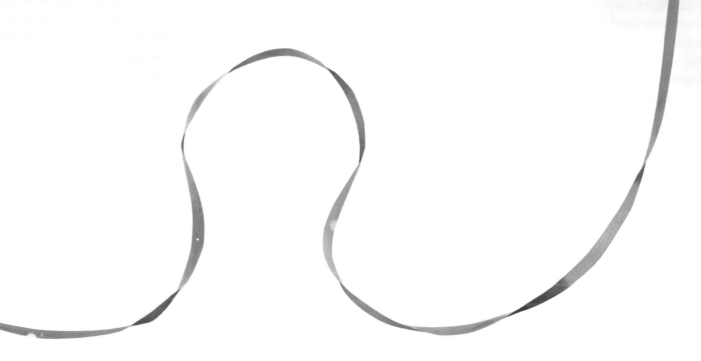

words & pictures

ONCE EVERY YEAR wishes take flight,
filled with hope and twinkling light.
They dance in the air, with a swirl and a swish,
you have to be lucky to be chosen by a wish.

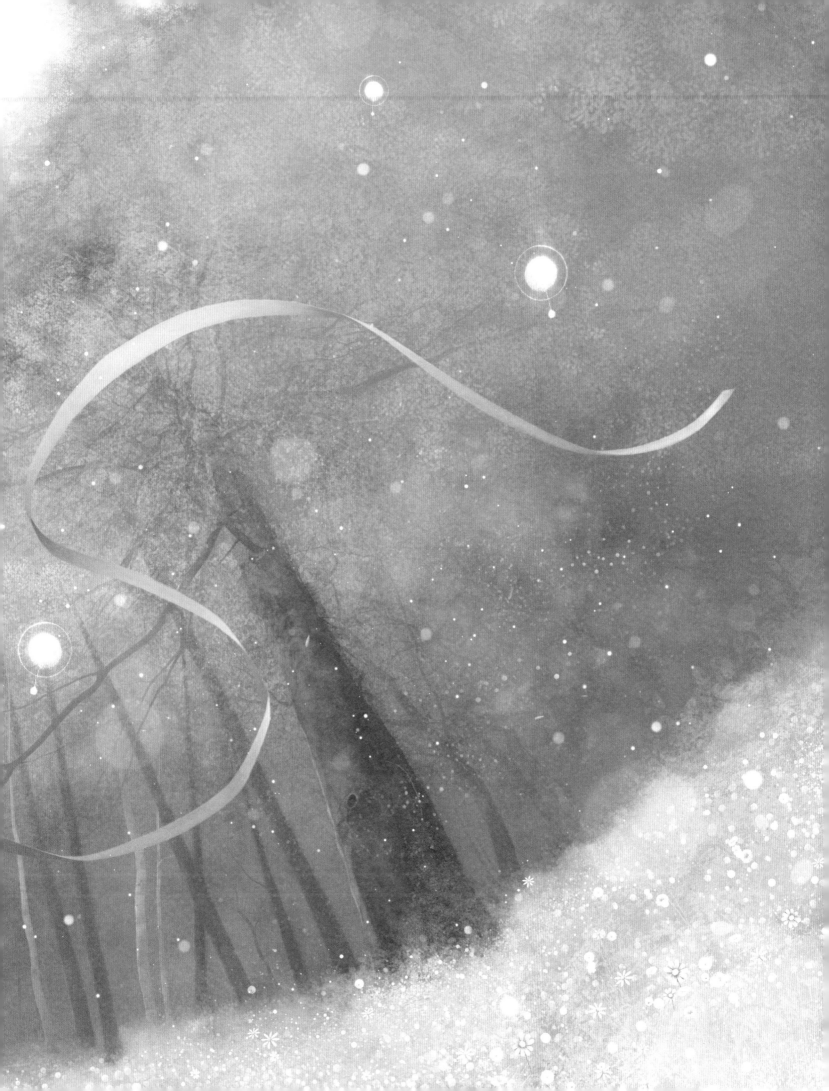

Rabbit was amazed as wishes danced and rose,
then all of a sudden, one landed on his nose!
Two more wishes fell at his feet,
now he had three, oh what a treat!

Rabbit had never caught a wish before,
he could not decide what to wish for.
So off Rabbit went with a hop and a swish,
to ask his friends what to do with a wish.

Rabbit asked Mouse:

"What would you wish for?"
His friend climbed up from the woodland floor.
"The world is big and I feel so small,
I wish I could fly, and see it all."

Rabbit looked to the sky...
what would they see?
And he thought to himself:
"Is this wish for me?"

So off Rabbit went with a hop and a swish,
to ask his friends what to do with a wish.

Rabbit asked Fox:

"What would you wish for?"
Wondering what his friend had in store.
"I wish I could write stories everyone would admire.
Books of knowledge and hope, and power to inspire."

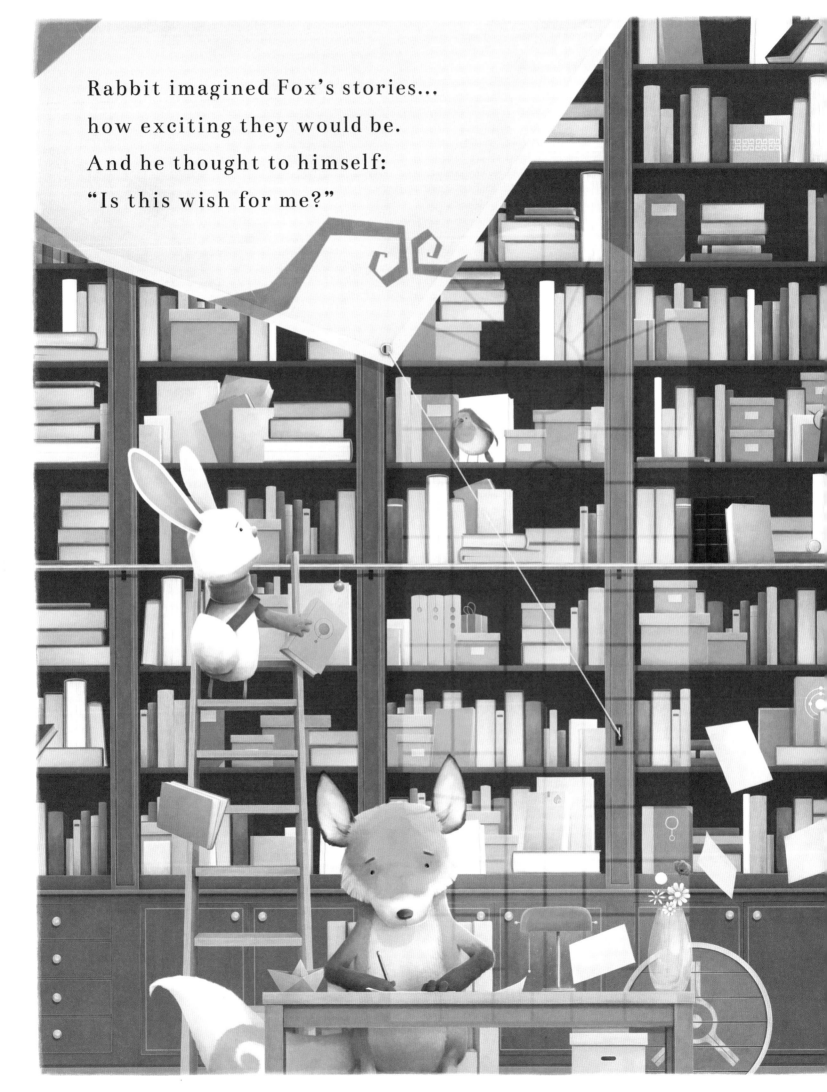

Rabbit imagined Fox's stories...
how exciting they would be.
And he thought to himself:
"Is this wish for me?"

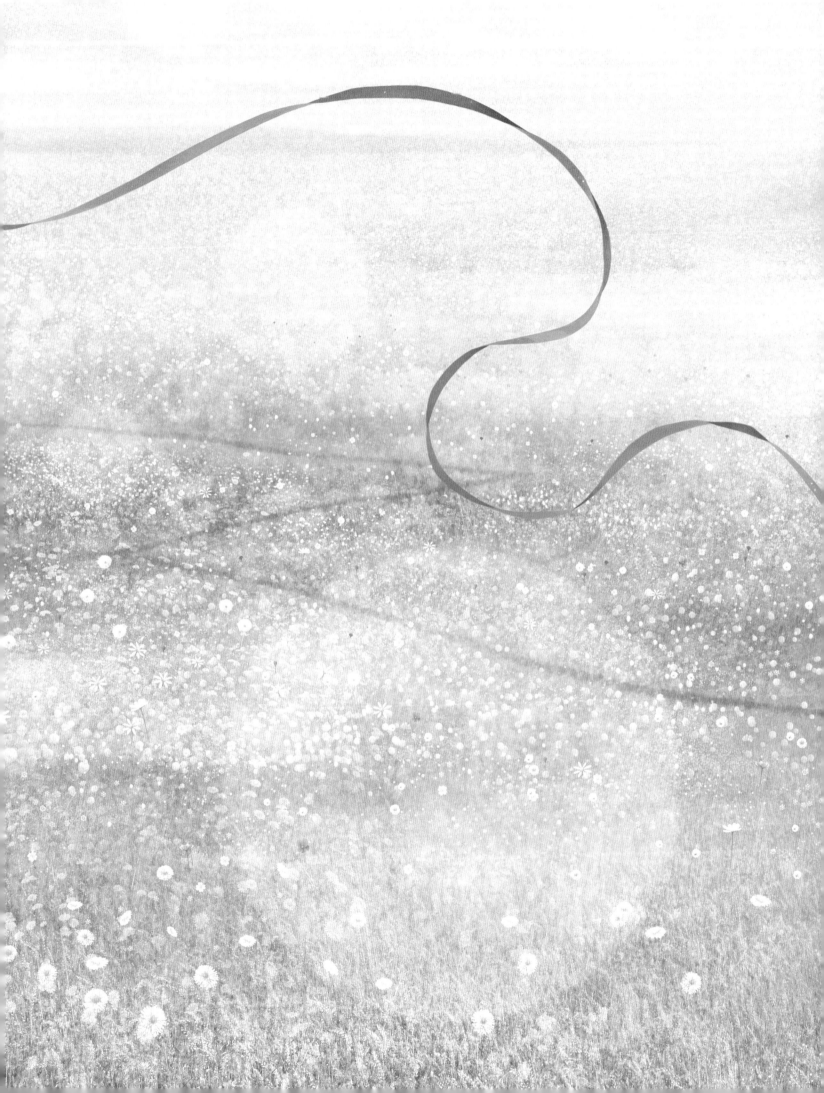

So off Rabbit went with a hop and a swish,
to ask his friends what to do with a wish.

Rabbit asked Bear:

"What would you wish for?"

As Bear watched the waves roll up the seashore.

"I have travelled over the mountains,
and climbed every rock and tree,
but I wish I had a boat to explore the open sea."

Rabbit wondered about the rowing,
and how strong Bear must be,
and he thought to himself:
"Is this wish for me?"

And now, still never having made a wish before, he finally asked himself: "What should *I* wish for?"

I wish for the small
to feel uplifted and tall.

I wish for inspiration
to wash over us all.

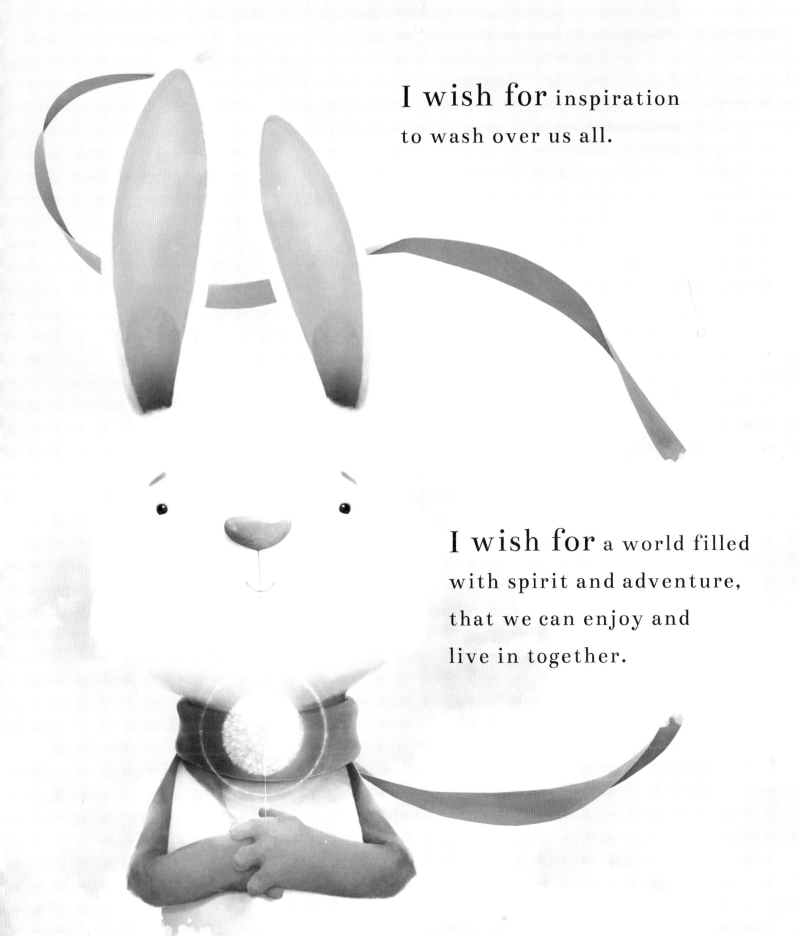

I wish for a world filled
with spirit and adventure,
that we can enjoy and
live in together.

So Rabbit granted his friends' wishes:
one, two and three!
Then he suddenly realised:
"There are none left for me!"

"Thank you, Rabbit for being so kind.
We have something to say,
if you don't mind?"

"By noticing me, you helped me feel tall,
treating me as your equal, even though I am small.

So if you find yourself lost,
forgotten or alone,
just look to the sky
and I will guide you home."

"Thanks to you I am busy writing.
Creating amazing stories so wonderfully exciting!

I have been inspired
by your selfless deed.
Please, choose a story
you wish me to read."

"I finally have a boat with which I can explore,
over the horizon, beyond the sandy shore.
But before I go, there is something you should see,
if you have a moment, please come with me..."

Bear asked Rabbit to close his eyes,
as he had a special surprise...

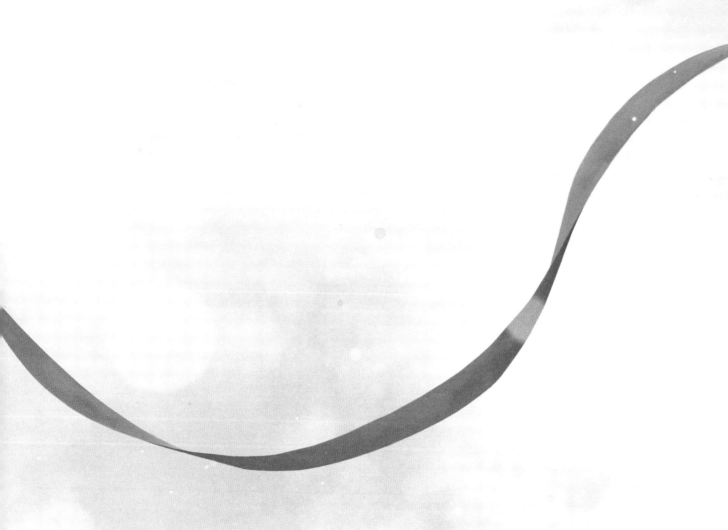

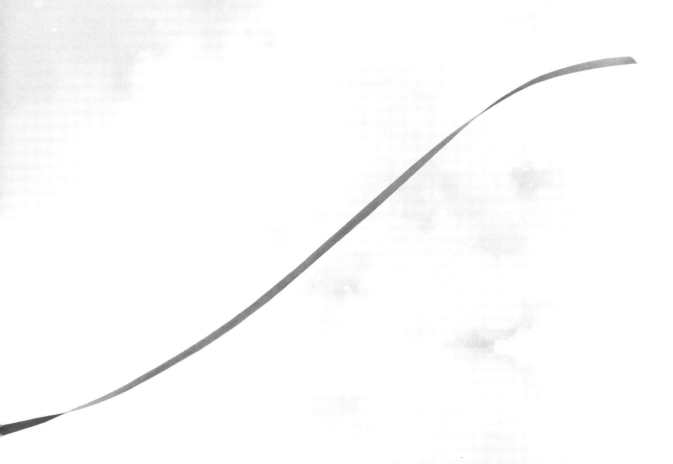

"It is never too late
to go on an adventure.
Thanks to you, little Rabbit
we can all go together."